Big Cat The Proud

Waterston Productions, Inc.
115 N.W. Oregon • Suite 8
Bend, Oregon 97701

ISBN #0-9628129-7-8

Library of Congress Catalog Card Number 91-65488

BIG CAT
THE PROUD

Written and Illustrated by Molly Pearce

Big Cat thought he was the biggest, strongest bulldozer that ever was.

Big Cat could push huge rocks
up into a pile
or down a mountain.

Big Cat was so proud
that he did not talk
to the others on the job . . .

certainly not to JD, the little loader.

Why should he?
All JD did was scoop up little loads
of small rocks
and put them in the dumptrucks.

The loaders and dumptrucks were friends,
but Big Cat
didn't speak to any of them.

One day all the machines were busy working.
The loaders were loading rocks,
the dumptrucks were dumping rocks,
and Big Cat was pushing rocks
up a steep mountain into an enormous pile.

"I am the biggest, strongest
'Dozer in the world!"
bragged Big Cat
as his pile got higher and higher.

"Look at me!" he shouted,
"I am the greatest!"

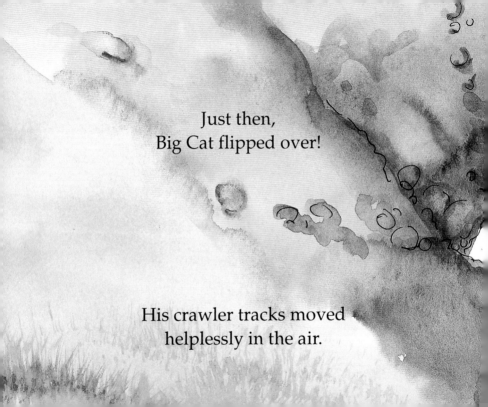

Just then,
Big Cat flipped over!

His crawler tracks moved
helplessly in the air.

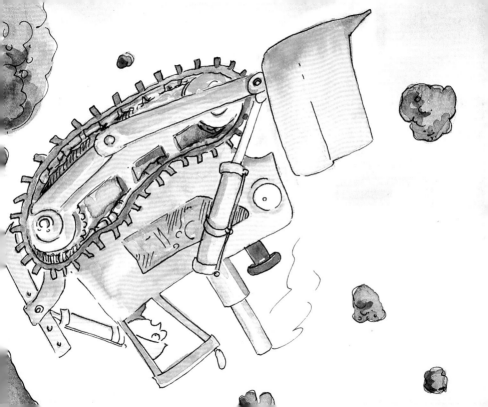

The dumptrucks and loaders
all saw Big Cat was in trouble,
but only JD hurried to help.

JD put his front-end loader under Big Cat
and gave a mighty shove, tipping Big Cat back up.

Big Cat felt very good to be right-side up again!

JD didn't look so puny to Big Cat now.

"Thanks, Buddy!" Big Cat said.

After that day,
Big Cat did not brag anymore –
and he always had a friendly word for JD.